This Book

Belongs To

____

____

Made in the USA
Monee, IL
29 March 2021

64166007R00059